i'M wiTH SiLLY

By lala

First published in India in 2016 by Harper Kids
An imprint of HarperCollins *Publishers*

Text and Illustrations © Khushnaz Lala 2016

P-ISBN: 978-93-5264-118-5
E-ISBN: 978-93-5264-119-2

2 4 6 8 10 9 7 5 3 1

Khushnaz Lala asserts the moral right to be identified as
the author and the illustrator of this work.

This is a work of fiction and all characters and incidents described in this
book are the product of the author's imagination. Any resemblance to
actual persons, living or dead, is entirely ~~coincidental.~~

Silly

HarperCollins *Publishers*

A-75, Sector 57, Noida, Uttar Pradesh 201301, India
1 London Bridge Street, London, SE1 9GF, United Kingdom
Hazelton Lanes, 55 Avenue Road, Suite 2900, Toronto, Ontario M5R 3L2
and 1995 Markham Road, Scarborough, Ontario M1B 5M8, Canada
25 Ryde Road, Pymble, Sydney, NSW 2073, Australia
195 Broadway, New York, NY 10007, USA

Printed and bound at Thomson Press (India) Ltd

i'm with SILLY

By Lala

HARPER KIDS

I'm with silly.

It seems like everyone
I'm surrounded by is

very

Very

VERY

silly.

Don't say I didn't warn you...

This is _____.

She likes to pretend
she's a chicken,
but really,
she's just a
silly goose.

———————— and ————————

like to wear their
parents' clothes.

They have tea parties
and give themselves
fancy names that
I can't spell.
But I call them silly.

This is a pair of
seven-fingered gloves.

How silly!
Who needs
seven-fingered gloves?

They were on sale,
so I bought them
anyway.

_____ invented his
own language.

He even made a
dictionary for it.
But he never ever
lets anyone read it.

He's so silly!

This is a
skateboarding snail.

Silly snail!
You can't skateboard,
you're a snail!

This is _____.

He spells his name
with a
silent number 6.

What a silly boy!

_____ claims he
has spoken to
aliens.

But that's a silly fib.

They told me that
they have never even
seen him before!

This is a large canvas
with a dot on it.

It's called art.
I think it's absolutely
ridiculous.

Ridiculous is another
word for silly.

This is a giant rock
floating around in
space.

It's full of silly
things...

... like talking monkeys
who believe they
control it.

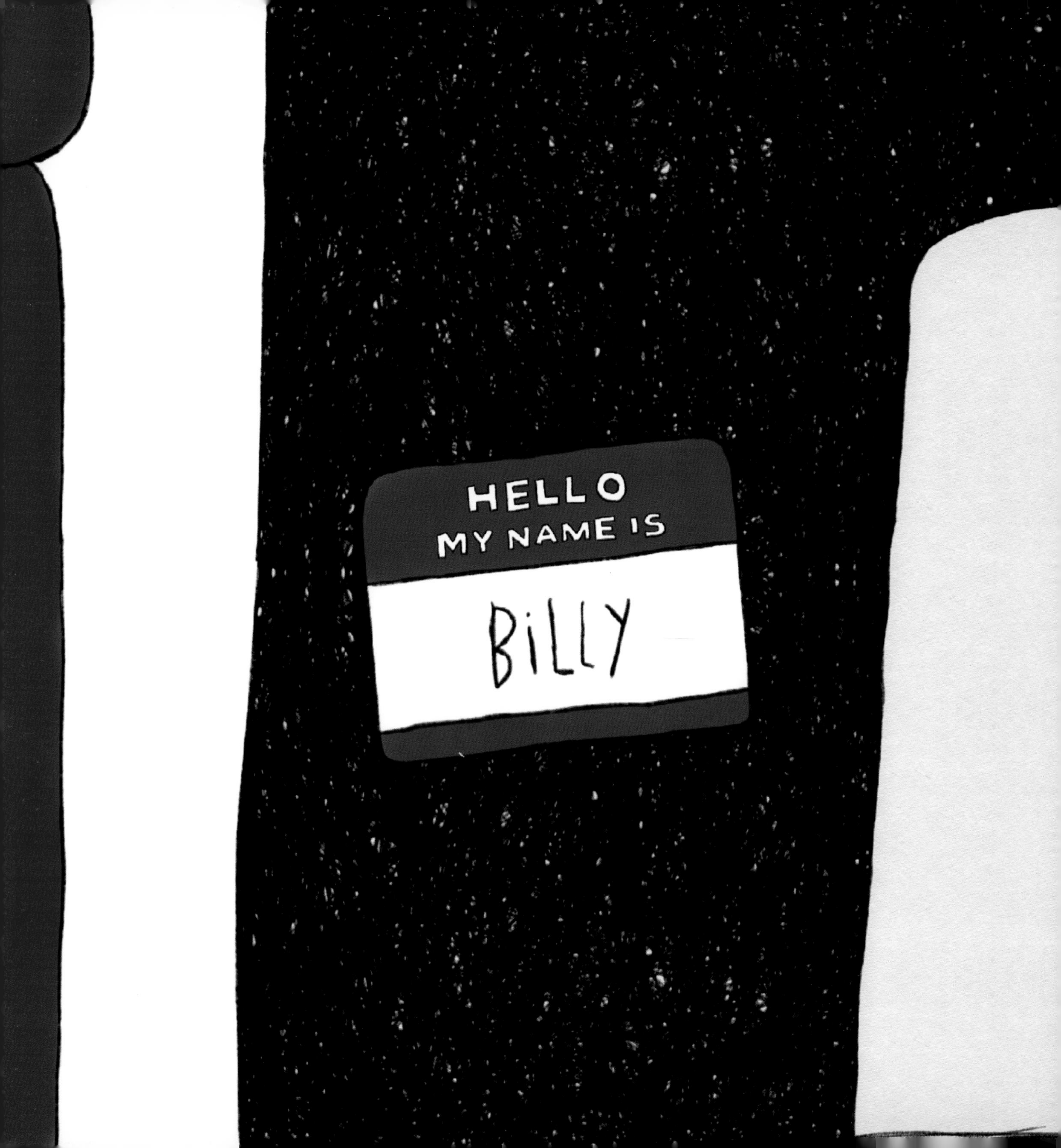
HELLO
MY NAME IS
BiLLY

They think this
world is serious.

They are the
SILLIEST
of all!

With quirky illustrations that will touch children and adults alike, here are three picture books that are perfect for fans of Oliver Jeffers.